W9-APW-763

A GOLDEN BOOK • NEW YORK

 Published in the United States by Golden Books, an imprint of Random House Children's Books, a division of Random House LLC, 1745 Broadway, New York, NY 10019, and in Canada by Random House of Canada Limited, Toronto, Penguin Random House Companies. The stories contained in this work were originally published separately by Golden Books as follows: *It's Time for Bubble Puppy!* and *The Doctor Is In!*, in 2012; and *Bubble Pirates!*, in 2013.

randomhousekids.com
ISBN 978-0-553-52115-3
MANUFACTURED IN MALAYSIA
10 9 8 7 6 5 4 3 2 1

nickelodeon
BUBBLE GUPPIES
IT'S TIME FOR BUBBLE PUPPY!

One morning, Gil was on his way to school when he heard barking.

"I hear puppies!" he said.

ARF!
ARF!
ARF!
ARF!
ARF!

Gil followed the barks and found a whole *bunch* of puppies!

"These puppies are up for adoption," explained a friendly lady snail. "That means we're looking for people to take them home and give them nice places to live."

"I wish I had a puppy like that one," Gil said, pointing to a cute little guy with orange spots that was barking happily. The puppy was friendly—and really good at chasing bubbles!

When Gil got to school, he told his friends Molly, Goby, Oona, Deema, and Nonny all about the puppy. "I wish I could adopt him," he said.

“Adopting a pet is a great thing to do,” said their teacher, Mr. Grouper. “You just have to find the right pet for you.”

“I want a cat that says *meow,*” said Molly.

“I want a parrot!” said Deema.

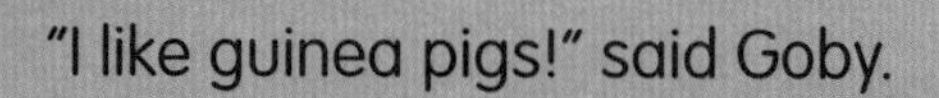

“I like guinea pigs!” said Goby.

"I think that puppy would be perfect for me," Gil said. "We'd be best buddies. He'd lick my face to wake me up every morning, and we would run and play in the park all the time!"

"But, Gil, you can't play with
the puppy all the time," Molly said.
"You have to take care of him, too."

"That's right," Mr. Grouper said.
"Taking care of a pet is a really big job."

"If your puppy is hungry, you'll have to give it food to eat," Mr. Grouper said.

"And puppies get thirsty, too, so they need lots of water," said Molly.

"And when your puppy needs to go outside," said Goby, "you'll put him on a leash and take him for a walk!"

"If that puppy was my pet, I would take really good care of him," said Gil.

"You would?" said Mr. Grouper. "Then come with me. Everybody, let's line up. I have something to show you!"

Mr. Grouper led the class through their watery world. Finally, they arrived at the puppy adoption center.

"This is where I met that puppy!" said Gil.

But when Gil looked for the puppies, they were all gone!

The lady snail told him that all the puppies had been adopted—including Gil's favorite! Gil was very sad.

"Here, you'll need these," said the lady snail, handing Gil a bowl and a leash.

"But why?" asked Gil.

"Because he's coming back to class with us!" said Mr. Grouper. "We adopted him!"

"Arf! Arf!" barked the happy little puppy.

All the Bubble Guppies cheered. "Yay! Thank you, Mr. Grouper!"

Everyone was very excited about their new pet.

They all agreed to help
take care of the new puppy.

"I'll give him
baths," said Gil.

"And I'll take him out for walks," said Goby.

Molly and Nonny couldn't wait to feed the puppy and give him water.

Oona said she would train the puppy.

"And I'll hug him!" promised Deema.

"But what should we call him?" asked Molly.

"Arf!" barked the puppy, and a big bubble came out of his mouth!

"I know," said Gil. "Let's call him . . . BUBBLE PUPPY!"

Everyone thought Bubble Puppy was a wonderful name. They all took turns hugging Bubble Puppy, and he licked them all back.

Gil gave Bubble Puppy a really big hug. "I'm glad we adopted you, boy," he said.

"Arf!" barked Bubble Puppy. He was happy to have a nice new home with all his new friends, the Bubble Guppies.

nickelodeon
BUBBLE GUPPIES
THE DOCTOR IS IN!

On her way to school one morning, Oona saw her friend Avi. He was riding his tricycle.

"Vroom! Vroom!" Avi said. "Look how fast I can go!"

Suddenly, Avi hit a rock and fell off his tricycle!
"Ow!" Avi cried. "Mommy, my tail fin hurts."

"You'll be okay, honey," said Avi's mommy. "But we'd better call the doctor, just to make sure."

Oona waved goodbye as Avi took a ride to the hospital with his mommy . . . in a clambulance.

When Oona got to class, she told everyone about Avi's accident.

"The doctor will take good care of him," said Mr. Grouper. "He'll probably take an X-ray."

"What's an X-ray?" Gil asked.

"An X-ray is a picture of your bones," said Nonny.

"Do we have bones?" Oona asked.

"You sure do, Guppies," Mr. Grouper said. "Bones are the hard things you feel under your skin. They help support and protect you.

"Without your bones, you
couldn't stand up,

jump,

or swim."

"I went to the doctor once," said Deema. "She made me stick out my tongue and say 'Ahhh!'"

"The doctor was checking your throat to make sure it was okay," said Mr. Grouper.

“What else do doctors do?” asked Oona.
“Let’s think about it,” said Mr. Grouper.

"Sometimes a doctor uses a special flashlight to look in your ear," said Oona.

"And sometimes a doctor will use a stethoscope to listen to your heart," said Gil.

"He or she will probably take your temperature with a thermometer," said Nonny.

"You might have to get a shot," said Deema.

"Shots hurt," said Nonny.

"Only a little bit," said Mr. Grouper. "But they keep you from getting sick."

"Oona, would you like to visit Avi in the hospital?" Mr. Grouper asked.

"We can bring him a balloon," Molly said.

Oona thought that was a great idea.

The Bubble Guppies lined up, and Mr. Grouper led them to the hospital. They saw doctors and nurses there, and patients who were getting better.

The Bubble Guppies and Mr. Grouper found Avi's room. Avi was in a big, comfy bed. His mother and his doctor were with him.

Avi was happy to see his friends. Everyone wanted to know how he was feeling.

"Avi will be fine," the doctor said. "He broke a bone in his tail fin, but we fixed him right up."

The doctor showed everyone Avi's X-ray.

And Avi showed everyone his cast! The doctor had put it on Avi's tail fin to help his bone heal.

"Who wants to sign my cast?" Avi asked.

The Bubble Guppies took turns signing their names and drawing pictures on Avi's cast.

When they were done, the doctor said Avi could go home!

"Let's pretend we're sick!" said Deema. *"Bleauuhhh!"*

"Oh no!" Mr. Grouper said, laughing. "I feel sick, too. Somebody call a clambulance!"

Mr. Grouper stuck out his tongue and turned green. All the Guppies thought this was really silly, and they laughed and laughed.

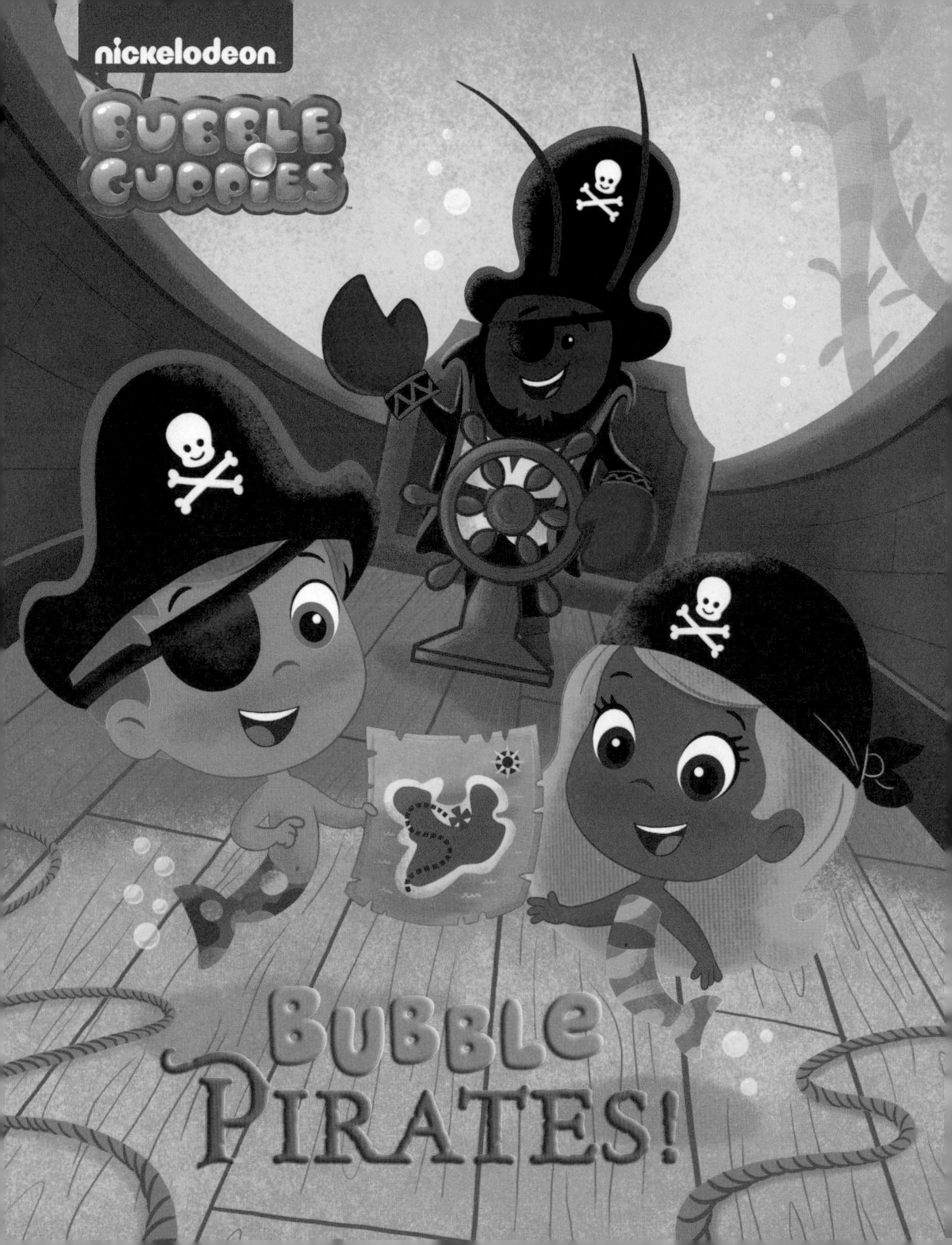
nickelodeon
BUBBLE GUPPIES
BUBBLE PIRATES!

Molly, Gil, and Bubble Puppy were on their way to school when they saw a pirate captain. He was digging in the sand.

"Are you digging for treasure?" asked Gil.

"Arrr!" said the pirate. "But I can't find it anywhere."

"X marks the spot," squawked the pirate's parrot.

"You keep saying that," grumbled the pirate. "But I can't find the X."

"Do you have a treasure map?" asked Gil.

"Of course I do," said the pirate. "But I don't understand it."

"Look!" exclaimed Molly. "There's an X."

"Aye, that's where the treasure is buried," explained the pirate.

"I wish I were a pirate," said Gil.
"Me too," added Molly.
"Arf! Arf!" said Bubble Puppy.

The pirate captain had an idea. If the Bubble Guppies helped him find the buried treasure, he would make them proper pirates and share the treasure with them.

Molly and Gil couldn't wait!

Molly and Gil quickly swam to school. When they got there, they told all the Bubble Guppies about the pirate they had met.

Everyone was excited—especially when they saw the treasure map.

"What are those pictures?" asked Oona.

"Those pictures show landmarks," explained Mr. Grouper. "Landmarks are things to look for along the way."

"Landmarks help you know where you are," added Nonny.

"And the X tells you where the treasure is buried!" added Gil.

Gil and Molly told their friends that if they could help find the treasure, the pirate would make them proper pirates for sure!

"Everyone who wants to be a pirate, say *'Arrr!'*" called Mr. Grouper.

"Arrr!" everyone shouted.

But Gil knew that to be proper pirates, they had to look like pirates.

So he swam over to Deema's Proper Pirate Store, where he found big pirate hats and awesome eye patches for everyone.

Now Gil and his pirate crew were ready to search for treasure.

They looked at the treasure map. The first landmark on the map was called Spyglass Peak.

Gil spotted a mountain shaped like a spyglass. "That's Spyglass Peak!" he yelled. "Come on!"

After Spyglass Peak, the pirates worked their way to the second landmark on the map, Buccaneer Bridge.

"Careful, mateys! This is Buccaneer Bridge, and it's a long way down!" Gil said nervously, glancing below.

The pirates slowly made their way across the creaky bridge.

"Look!" cried Molly. "There's Parrot Rock! That's our last landmark!"

"That means we're almost at the X," said Gil. "C'mon, mateys!"

When they reached the X, the Bubble Guppies started digging for the treasure.

They dug deep, deep down into the ground.

"We found the treasure!" exclaimed Gil.

Just then, the pirate captain arrived. "Ahoy, mateys!" he called.

"We followed the map and found the treasure!" Gil told the pirate.

The captain was so happy. He made Gil, Molly, and all the Bubble Guppies part of his crew.

"Hooray!" they shouted. "We're proper pirates!"

Gil and his friends climbed aboard the pirate ship.

"I promised to share the treasure with you if you found it," said the pirate captain. "You found where X marks the spot, so let's open the treasure chest to see what's inside, mateys!"

The chest was filled with something shiny and golden. It looked like a spoon—and also like a fork.

"It's called a spork," proclaimed the pirate. "X marks the spork!"

The Guppies laughed.

The Bubble Guppies sat down for lunch and passed out their golden sporks.

"What do pirates eat, anyway?" asked Molly.

"*Map*-aroni and cheese, of course!" exclaimed the pirate captain.

"*Arrr!*" agreed the Bubble Guppies.